The Big Box

A lesson on being honest

by Suzanne I. Barchers

illustrated by Mattia Cerato

RED
CHAIR
•PRESS•

Please visit our website at **www.redchairpress.com**.
Find a free catalog of all our high-quality products for young readers.

The Big Box
Library of Congress Control Number: 2012931800
ISBN: 978-1-937529-18-5 (pbk)
ISBN: 978-1-937529-26-0 (hc)

Lexile is a registered trademark of MetaMetrics, Inc. Used with permission.
Leveling provided by Linda Cornwell of Literacy Connections Consulting.

This edition first published in 2012 by
Red Chair Press, LLC   PO Box 333   South Egremont, MA 01258-0333

Printed in China
1 2 3 4 5 16 15 14 13 12

Bun

Pip

Sox

Tab

Ted

The Big Box

Tab and Sox find a treasure that doesn't belong to them. Should the friends keep the lost box and share the surprises inside? Or should the five friends try to find the owner and return the big box? What would you do?

One sunny day, Tab is strolling with Sox.
"Look!" says Sox. "Do you see that box?

I bet it fell off a delivery truck.
I guess it's ours now. That's really good luck!"

"What do you mean?" Tab says to Sox.
"We may have found it. But it's not our box.

Someone must miss it. They may feel sad.
If I lost a box, I'd feel bad."

"Hi guys," says Pip. She's with Ted and Bun.
"What are you doing? Are you out for a run?"

"We are out for a walk," says Tab. "How are you?
We found this big box and don't know what to do."

"I see a word," says Bun. "Is it a clue?
Maybe it tells who the box belongs to."

Ted says, "I can read it. It just says *Pops*. Maybe it belongs to one of the shops."

"I saw it first," Sox says. "I'll decide.
No one will miss it. Let's take it inside.

Whatever it is, we can each have a share.
Let's all just keep it. No one will care."

Tab says with a frown, "Let's think this through.
I don't think that is the right thing to do.

14

We just need to know who it really goes to.
Perhaps the word *Pops* can give us a clue."

"Maybe it's popcorn. Popcorn goes pop!
I love eating popcorn!" Bun says with a hop.

"Some books pop up. That would be fun.
We'd read the books first and share them when done."

"What if it's lollipops? That would be sweet.
This box weighs a lot. We'd all get a treat!"

"Some toys go pop. I like those a lot.
What should we do? We're in a tough spot."

"I think we should take the box into town.
You may disagree," Tab says with a frown.

"Look! *Pops* is a name," Bun says with a smile.
"I bet he was looking for this for a while!"

They give the box to the kindly old bear.
"Thank you," he says. "I am glad that you care."

With the lid finally off Pops lets out a cheer.
"Balloons for the party I've been planning all year!"

"Here you go kids, each take one.
Now it is time to have some fun."

The friends are so happy they start to sing.
It always feels good when you do the right thing.

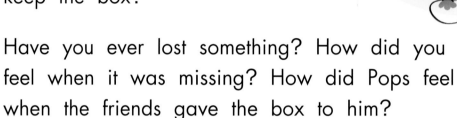

Big Questions:

Why does Tab tell Sox they cannot keep the box?

Have you ever lost something? How did you feel when it was missing? How did Pops feel when the friends gave the box to him?

Big Words:

clue: a fact to help solve a problem

decide: to make a choice

strolling: to enjoy a slow, easy walk

Sox wanted to keep the box. If you found something that did not belong to you, what would you do? Can you think of two people you could tell who might help you find the owner?

If you found a box with the clue "This side up" on it, what would you hope was inside?

With a friend or group of friends, play a game to guess what is inside a box. Each player takes a turn hiding an item in the box. The other players get to ask a question of the one who hid the item. Questions must be answered with a 'yes' or 'no.' For example, you ask "Is the item a food?" or "Is the item a banana?" Keep asking about more clues until someone guesses correctly what is in the box.

About the Author

Suzanne I. Barchers, Ed.D., began a career in writing and publishing after fifteen years as a teacher. She has written over 100 children's books, two college textbooks, and more than 20 reader's theater and teacher resource books. She previously held editorial roles at Weekly Reader and LeapFrog and is on the PBS Kids Media Advisory Board for the next generation of children's programming. Suzanne also plays the flute professionally—and for fun—from her home in Stanford, CA.

About the Illustrator

Mattia Cerato was born in Cuneo, a small town in northern Italy where he still lives and works. As soon as he could hold a pencil he loved sketching things he saw around him. When he is not drawing, Mattia loves traveling around the world, reading good books, and playing and listening to cool music.

For a free activity page for this story, go to www.redchairpress.com and look for Free Activities.